Paramedic Chris

Episode 2

A Helping Hand

Tim Parsons

New Generation Publishing

Acknowledgements

This book is dedicated to my family, especially to my wife Caroline and two sons, William and Daniel. A special thanks must also go to Ann Hoare, who has been an inspiration to myself.

I also would like to thank my work colleagues at South East Coast Ambulance Service, who are all remarkable people and a special thanks to Chris Treves and Craig Martin for their medical input for writing this book.

A thanks to the following colleagues for allowing me the experience of observing their work, which has enabled me to write the Paramedic Chris stories: Kim, Kay, Margaret, Fiona, Charlotte, Karen, Liam and Mary.

A Helping Hand

One winter's day Paramedic Chris was talking to his team at Shadesdon Station; Sheldon, Zara and Holly.

"These winter months can leave us with big problems," Paramedic Chris began.

"What do you mean?" Sheldon asked.

"Well, you see the winter months can be very miserable and many people can become very lonely," stated Paramedic Chris.

"Are there any things we can do to help people this winter?" asked Zara.

Before Paramedic Chris could answer this question, a call came through on the radio to attend to a patient who was unwell.

Paramedic Chris was teamed with Holly and they left the station in an Ambulance.

It was raining heavily on their journey to the patient, who lived in Shadesdon, which made the journey even longer.

When they arrived at the address, Holly knocked on the patient's door, but there was no answer. Holly took a look through the letterbox and shouted, "Is anybody there? It is the Ambulance Service."

After a few minutes, a gentleman appeared in view and came slowly to the door.

When the gentleman answered the door, Holly and Paramedic Chris followed the gentleman to a dark and cluttered front room. The blue curtains were half-draping down and it did not look like the room had been cleaned for a very long time, as it was very dirty and untidy.

"How can we be of assistance this morning?" Holly asked.

"As you can see, I use walking sticks to get around, due to my health." Chris noticed the gentleman was very upset.

"We are really sorry to hear this, we will do our best to help you this morning," Holly answered.

Meanwhile, Paramedic Chris was getting out various bits of equipment from his observation kit.

"What is your name?"

"My name is Fred" Fred replied meekly.

"Do you mind if we do some checks, Fred?" asked Paramedic Chris.

"No problem."

Paramedic Chris undertook all the observations: blood pressure, heart rate, breathing rate, temperature and blood sugar.

"Would you like me to put the kettle on?" Holly asked Fred, to which he was very grateful.

***

Paramedic Chris, Holly and Fred had a warm drink each, sitting on the ripped sofa.

"How long have you lived here for?" Paramedic Chris asked Fred.

"I have lived here for thirty years now but, ever since my wife died, I have not gone out much," Fred replied.

"You see, I struggle to walk, and I just read the paper each day and watch television. I have no family; I cry most of the time as I have nobody to talk to".

"Do you have any carers come and help?" Holly questioned.

"I have no carers as I do not know who to ask… if I am honest, I was a bit ashamed to ask," Fred replied.

"We can assist you with this today, Fred," Holly said.

"If you could excuse me for a minute, Fred, I am going to make a telephone call to the appropriate people to get you the support you need," said Paramedic Chris.

While Paramedic Chris was on his mobile, Holly was chatting to Fred about his job and his wife, and Fred started to smile, "This is the first time I have smiled in a long time, or chatted to anybody," Fred said.

Paramedic Chris finished on the phone, "I have some good news for you, Fred."

"I have arranged for a visit from a community support worker for tomorrow, who will come and chat to you about how they can help you".

"That is good news," Fred replied.

Paramedic Chris looked in Fred's kitchen cupboards to make sure he had food in to cook for himself. The cupboard was empty, apart from a few teabags, stale bread and sugar.

"Do you have any food, Fred?" Chris asked.

Fred looked down at his hands. "I haven't had the money or strength to do a big food shop this week."

Paramedic Chris radioed into the station and requested that they stay with the patient longer.

"Why did you do that?" Fred asked Paramedic Chris.

"I did this because I am going to give you a food bank voucher and see if we can make sure you get the help you need," Paramedic Chris replied.

"I do not have any money here," Fred stated.

"No problem, Fred. The food bank is free," Paramedic Chris replied.

Fred started to cry and said to Paramedic Chris and Holly, "You cannot do that as I am wasting your time when you could go to other emergencies," Fred said.

"You're not a waste of time Fred, if we can help in this way, we are doing our job by caring for you," Holly said.

Paramedic Chris went and bought a loaf of bread and a pint of milk from the local shop and explained to Fred all about the food bank and how the volunteers could help him until his money came in from his pension.

"What are you doing?" Fred asked Paramedic Chris as Chris was in the kitchen.

"I am making you some toast and another hot drink," Paramedic Chris replied.

Fred started to cry again. "I have never had anybody treat me so nicely as this before in all of my life. I cannot understand why you are caring so much for me."

"Fred, you need to learn to like yourself as you're a lovely gentleman," Holly said.

"I know what you're saying, but I really do get down being stuck in this house," Fred replied.

"That is why we have organised for somebody to come and visit tomorrow to start to look at how others can help you," Paramedic Chris replied.

"When they come tomorrow, Fred, make sure you let them know that you need to go out more but you need support to do that. There are many things that you can do, for example, lunch clubs and transport can be arranged," Holly said.

"What a wonderful idea," Fred replied.

"We must go now, Fred, as we have had another call come through, but we are delighted to see you are smiling now," Paramedic Chris said.

"Thank you very much both of you; when you came today, I was very upset, feeling like no one cared, and now I feel so much better because you have given me hope," Fred said.

Holly and Paramedic Chris were delighted that they were able to help Fred and get him the support he needed.

A few weeks later, a card was sent to the station for Paramedic Chris and Holly. Opening it, Paramedic Chris read out loud to all the crew members:

To Paramedic Chris and Holly.

Thank you for coming and helping me when I was not feeling well. The next day Dorothy came round, as she is a community support worker, and she has arranged for me to go out every Wednesday with the over 60's, and I am now walking outside more every day and have made a number of friends.

Yours Fred.

"What a lovely card, Chris," said Zara.
"Yes, it shows what you say and do can make a real difference."

To Paramedic Chris and Holly,

Thank you for coming and helping me when I was not feeling well. The next day Dorothy came round as she is a community support worker and she has arranged for me to go out every wednesday with the over 60's and I am now walking out more each day and have made a number of friends.

Yours, Fred

Milton Keynes UK
Ingram Content Group UK Ltd.
UKHW050314130224
437742UK00003B/104